Put Beginning Readers on the Right Track with
ALL ABOARD READING™

The All Aboard Reading series is especially designed for beginning readers. Written by noted authors and illustrated in full color, these are books that children really want to read—books to excite their imagination, expand their interests, make them laugh, and support their feelings. With fiction and nonfiction stories that are high interest and curriculum-related, All Aboard Reading books offer something for every young reader. And with four different reading levels, the All Aboard Reading series lets you choose which books are most appropriate for your children and their growing abilities.

Picture Readers
Picture Readers have super-simple texts, with many nouns appearing as rebus pictures. At the end of each book are 24 flash cards—on one side is a rebus picture; on the other side is the written-out word.

Station Stop 1
Station Stop 1 books are best for children who have just begun to read. Simple words and big type make these early reading experiences more comfortable. Picture clues help children to figure out the words on the page. Lots of repetition throughout the text helps children to predict the next word or phrase—an essential step in developing word recognition.

Station Stop 2
Station Stop 2 books are written specifically for children who are reading with help. Short sentences make it easier for early readers to understand what they are reading. Simple plots and simple dialogue help children with reading comprehension.

Station Stop 3
Station Stop 3 books are perfect for children who are reading alone. With longer text and harder words, these books appeal to children who have mastered basic reading skills. More complex stories captivate children who are ready for more challenging books.

In addition to All Aboard Reading books, look for All Aboard Math Readers™ (fiction stories that teach math concepts children are learning in school); All Aboard Science Readers™ (nonfiction books that explore the most fascinating science topics in age-appropriate language); and All Aboard Poetry Readers™ (funny, rhyming poems for readers of all levels).

All Aboard for happy reading!

TO

Bianca & Madeline

A dog who thinks she's a cat,
and a cat who puts up with her.—M C-L

Copyright © 2004 by Maryann Cocca-Leffler. All rights reserved. Published by Grosset & Dunlap, a division of Penguin Young Readers Group, 345 Hudson Street, New York, New York 10014. GROSSET & DUNLAP and ALL ABOARD READING are trademarks of Penguin Group (USA) Inc. Printed in the U.S.A.

ISBN 978-0-448-43370-7   17 19 20 18 16

ALL ABOARD READING™

DOG WASH DAY

By Maryann Cocca-Leffler

Grosset & Dunlap • New York

Today is  wash day.

We have a big

for the big .

And a small

for the small .

We have

and

and lots of .

Our little brother

wants to help.

"No!" we say.

We put on

and  .

All we need now

are some  .

So we make  .

We put our

in a  .

We call,

"We will wash

today!"

Soon, lots of

show up.

Lulu looks like a

with a .

Buster looks like

he has a black .

Holly looks like a

with a .

Lulu

Buster

Holly

More  come.

There are

with short .

There are

with .

Our brother wants to

get into the , too.

"No!" I say.

"Today, this

is for ,

not a !"

We wash the  .

We dry them

with ![towels] .

They are nice

and clean.

My brother is back.

He has our .

Oh, no!

There goes the .

There go the .

There goes our brother.

They run

into the .

They jump over the .

They go under the .

Oh, no!

What a mess.

Today is  wash day.

Today is wash day, too!

pool	tub
dogs	dog
shampoo	towels

water	raincoats
boots	signs
wagon	mop

bow	eye
hot dog	tail
ears	spots

boy	cat
fence	brush
flowers	clothes